PIRATES AHOY!

Hans Wilhelm

Parents Magazine Press
New York

A Parents Magazine
Read Aloud Original

Library of Congress Cataloging-in-Publication Data

Wilhelm, Hans, 1945–
Pirates ahoy! / by Hans Wilhelm.
    p.   cm.
Summary: Bored farm animals turn different
vehicles into pirate ships to create excitement.
ISBN 0-8193-1162-6
[1. Domestic animals—Fiction.   2. Pirates—
Fiction.]   I. Title.
PZ7.W64816Pi   1987
[E]—dc 19   87-30197
                                                              CIP

To the child in all of us

It was a slow morning on the farm.
All the animals were bored.
There was nothing to do.
Nothing at all…

…until Fletcher found
something interesting.
"Look!" he called.
"I found an old wagon.
Let's take it for a ride!"

The wagon became their rumbly,
bumbly pirate ship.

The pirates began to go
faster and faster.
"Here we come!" they cried.
"The world is ours!"

They made it only to a
big old apple tree.
But they didn't give up.
Fletcher saw something new
coming down the road.

A schoolbus became a big,
bouncy pirate ship.

Being a pirate is hard work.
Pirates and school children must eat.
So, everyone had ice cream.

The bus really wasn't
fast enough, so...

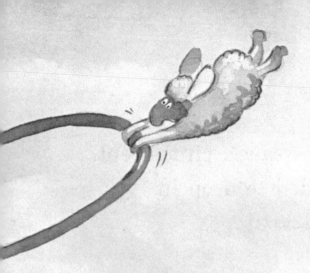

...a fire engine became a speeding, clanging pirate ship.

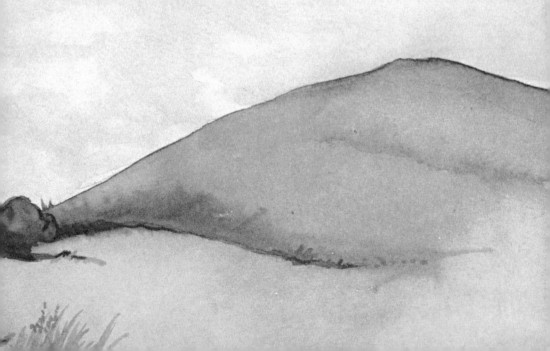

The pirates saw a circus tent.
They decided to drop in
for a short visit.

They put on a show of their own.

The lions were as surprised as the audience.

But pirates need a ship,
not a circus.
So they set out to find
the best one they could.

A plane became a looping,
swooping pirate ship.

But after a few loops they felt dizzy.
They decided it was time to land.

And so they did.

They were right back on the farm.
In no time, they were bored again.
There was nothing to do.
Nothing at all…

About the Author

Hans Wilhelm has written and illustrated
over fifty children's books, which have
been published around the world. He makes
his home in Westport, Connecticut.

Some of Mr. Wilhelm's best friends are pigs
—so he's a vegetarian.